The Adventures
of
Mr. H Hogg.

By Alex Fisher

Grosvenor House
Publishing Limited

This book is published by
Grosvenor House Publishing Ltd
Link House
140 The Broadway, Tolworth, Surrey, KT6 7HT.
www.grosvenorhousepublishing.co.uk

This book is a work of fiction. Any resemblance to
people or events, past or present, is purely coincidental.

A CIP record for this book
is available from the British Library

ISBN 978-1-80381-518-3

For my family.

Acknowledgements

I would like to thank my family and Katie for their endless support when I write and even when I'm not.

I would like to thank all the primary school teachers who took the time to read my manuscript, and all others who gave my work a read and gave their valued feedback.

I would like to thank Grosvenor House Publishing for taking my work on to be published and for guiding me through the process.

Chapter 1

Our story begins in the least likely of places. A pile of brown, rotten leaves from last autumn may not look like much to me, or to you, but to Mr. H Hogg, as he was known around the forest, this pile of brown, rotten leaves was home.

But now, with daylight beginning to stretch, and the birds beginning to sing a glorious chorus, there was change in the air. There were blossoms on the trees and the forest awakened from its long slumber as spring arrived. Within the pile of brown leaves, someone else stirred too.

With a yawn, Mr. Hogg pulled himself up from his pillow and sat on the edge of his bed and wondered how winter could have passed so quickly. Everyone in the forest knew, as you must too, how much Mr. Hogg loved his home. It was cosy and warm, always full of food and welcome. He did not leave it, or the forest, much – and certainly not for adventures.

Stretching his arms and legs, and bristles, he reached over to his bedside table and put on his large, round glasses. Something is not right here, he thought, something has changed since I went to sleep. So, he cleaned his glasses and put them back on, checking his sight was not tricking him. Confused, he leaned in for a closer look.

An egg? An egg! 'What is an egg doing here?' asked Mr. Hogg. 'Someone must have lost their egg!'

Was it a bird's egg? A duck's egg?
A pheasant? A lizard? Or a snake? His
bristles rattled and he tried not to ball up
at the thought of a snake being inside his
home whilst he was asleep. It was a large
white egg with brown spots. There was
nothing mysterious about it, apart from
its location. He picked it up, surprised
by its weight, and considered: perhaps
I should leave it outside and hopefully
the owner will return for it? I would
hate to think whoever has lost their egg

would think of me as a thief! So, he sat
at his table and had breakfast to settle his
mind. Strangely enough, he could feel
the egg staring at him, and he stared
at the egg, all lost and alone, and decided
then and there with a fist upon the table:
'I must help whoever has lost their egg!
I am a creature of the forest and creatures
of the forest must help each other.'

Donning his hat and grabbing his
walking stick, he stepped out of the
front door. The light outside was bright
and he shielded his eyes, but the spring
forest was beautiful. Blossoms covered
the tips of the trees and green shoots
sprouted from the forest floor. Birds
sang as they flew from branch to
branch, and the world smelled of new
beginnings. He would have enjoyed a
morning stroll, but he had a mission to
complete. A stroll could wait. 'I shan't
be long.' said Mr. Hogg.

Walking as fast as his furry feet could carry him (which wasn't too fast at all) he tracked the paths of the forest floor that he knew best, heading for the tall trees that birds tended to nest in.

One such path passed by a very old oak tree with a small painted door at the base of the trunk. Snowdrops bloomed around the long twisting roots, amongst the other splashes of colour from the other early flowers, almost making a pathway to the door. Raking the dead winter litter from the vegetable plots, was the owner of such a beautiful abode. Rabbit was and always had been an excellent gardener. Flowers grew all year, and vegetables were grown, harvested and tended to with expert care. 'Good morning, Mr. Hogg!' Rabbit called.

'Good morning, Rabbit.' Mr. Hogg replied as he walked.

'How was your hibernation this year?' asked Rabbit.

'Too short, my dear fellow, too short!' replied Mr. Hogg and they laughed at the common joke.

'I hope you don't mind me asking, Mr. Hogg, but whatever do you have in your paws?' asked Rabbit.

Mr. Hogg stopped and showed Rabbit the egg and how it came to be. 'I am on a mission to return it to its parent, whomever it may be. I am sure they are terribly worried. You may join me if you'd like?' he asked, hoping for companionship after the long and lonesome winter months.

Rabbit smiled and nodded to his friend, then thumped his foot in irritation. 'How excellent! I would love to join your quest! Although, I am rather busy, I have much to do to prepare for spring: starting with this leaf litter! It's wonderful to live beneath a tree, but it does make one's garden rather messy.'

Mr. Hogg understood, although he liked the leaf litter – it reminded him of home. 'I can help with that, if you would like?'

'Of course! Only if it's not interfering with your day or would be too much trouble. I am sure I keep a spare rake around here somewhere.'

Mr. Hogg set the egg down against the tree and removed his hat, folding his glasses. 'There is no need for a rake, my friend.' He popped himself into a spiky ball and rolled up and down the vegetable plot, the leaves sticking onto his spines until the plot was completely clear!

Rabbit clapped and hopped in joy, 'excellent! Thank you! No need for a rake, indeed. You are the rake!' laughed Rabbit as Mr. Hogg, now a ball of brown leaves, unfurled himself and laughed too.

'These prickles come in handy from time to time!' replied Mr. Hogg, donning his hat and picking up the egg.

'Well now, since my garden is beautiful thanks to your wonderful spines, I can join you, if you'll have me?' asked Rabbit.

'Of course!' replied Mr. Hogg.

Rabbit collected his waistcoat and walking stick and they both took to the path that led to the tall trees where the birds nested. They strolled through the undergrowth, following the path that led up a slope, winding around moss-covered rocks until they came upon trees that were so tall, they could not see the tops, and could only see dark bunches balanced in the branches. And as he resettled his glasses, Mr. Hogg saw they were nests.

The birds were singing loudly and flapping from branch to branch. At first, Mr. Hogg and Rabbit began to call out to them, to the pigeons and woodpeckers, to the ravens and the magpies, but each time they struggled to be heard, so they decided to find the lowest nest to make an inquiry, because, you see, despite being a wonderful song, too many songs at once can make one hard of hearing.

Walking around the trees, Mr. Hogg found a nest settled lower in a tree than others and called out to the bird. 'Hello! Forgive me for the intrusion of your home and the interruption of your song, but I was hoping you could help me? My name is Mr. H Hogg, and this is my good friend, Rabbit.'

Rabbit gave a bow.

There was a wait, until the bird, a large thrush, spotted them below over the edge of her nest. 'Hello, kind sirs!' sang the thrush, 'what is it that I can help you with?'

Holding the egg out for the thrush to see, Mr. Hogg explained the situation. 'I was hoping to discover whether you or any other of your fellow feathered friends have lost an egg? I would dearly like to return this poor thing to its parent.'

After joining a sweet melody from the neighbouring tree, there was a reply. 'How kind you are, Mr. H Hogg and

Rabbit!' sang the thrush, 'I have a friend nearby whose nest and eggs were knocked out of her tree during high winds, poor thing! She might be the owner of your lost egg.'

'Where might we find the bird with her fallen nest?' asked Rabbit.

Once the thrush had finished another song, she replied with, 'she is a robin, and she is near the large white birch tree.' With the feather of a wing, the thrush pointed in the direction they needed to go.

'Thank you ever so much!' cried Mr. Hogg and they marched in the direction that had been pointed. They passed many trees and pushed through many bushes until they found a large white birch with spindly branches and a broken nest lying scattered upon the forest floor. Perched in a low branch, was a crying robin. Her wings covered her eyes as she wept.

Mr. Hogg and Rabbit approached with care, and he spoke softly, removing his hat. 'My dear robin, we are terribly sorry for what has happened to your nest. I hope I may bring you solace in what I bring with me.' He showed her the egg, 'we were told you lost your eggs, and I believe I have found one. My name is Mr. H Hogg, and this is my dear friend, Rabbit.'

Rabbit gave a bow.

The robin wiped away a tear and sang a beautiful song of loss, and of hope, as she flapped down to the ground to meet them. She looked over the egg and placed a wing upon it. 'I thank you so much for your kindness, Mr. H Hogg. I have lost much recently but love and hope are things I still carry within my little red breast. Although, I am sorry to tell you that this is not my egg.'

Mr. Hogg placed his paw upon her wing. 'Ah. There is nothing to be sorry for. Even though this may not be your egg, we would still like to help you in your time of sorrow, if we can. Is there anything we can do?'

'Perhaps we could help to rebuild your nest?' suggested Rabbit.

Robin's eyes widened and she took off, flying with joy, returning with gratitude. 'Nothing could make me happier! How excellent that would be! Thank you!'

'Of course! What materials do you need?'

'Twigs and moss and leaves and spider's webs. I don't suppose you have these things at hand?' asked Robin.

'As a matter of fact, we do!' cried Mr. Hogg and he turned around, showing his back and his spines packed with leaves! Rabbit clapped in joy and Robin

flapped her wings with happiness.
Mr. Hogg gently placed the egg at the base of the tree, and it watched as, without delay, they set to work.

As Robin flew away to search for moss and spider webs, Rabbit picked the ground for twigs and began to set the nest, weaving the twigs together. Rabbit was an excellent gardener, as I have mentioned, and enjoyed weaving wicker baskets beside his fire. Mr. Hogg added leaves from his spines, and together they packed the materials until a rough shape formed. Robin returned and they added the moss, sticking everything together with the webs, and Rabbit, with his profoundly strong legs, pressed and packed and pushed everything together with a few powerful thumps. Robin then jumped in the center, and they padded the nest to her until the nest became the perfect size. Then,

after a leg and a wing, they managed to
climb the tree to a perfect branch, a spot
much more sheltered from high winds
and rough weather.

Robin then hopped in, nestled
down and closed her eyes and sang
the most beautiful song. 'Thank you,
oh thank you! You have given me
a new home and another chance
at a family. How can I ever repay
you?' asked Robin.

'There is no need for repayment, my dear robin. All I wish for is you to continue your sweet melody. Sing loudly and sing well and spread cheer to this forest and to the world with your wonderful song.' said Mr. Hogg. 'Although, I don't suppose I could ask if you would know to whom this egg of mine belongs to?'

'I'm very sorry to say that I don't know,' sang Robin, 'but I can tell you that it is not the egg of a bird.'

'Very well, we shall continue our quest. Farewell Robin, I wish you all the best for the nesting season.'

'Thank you so much for all you have done for me, Mr. H Hogg, and thank you Rabbit!'

Rabbit gave a bow. 'Of course. Goodbye.'

Carefully, they climbed down the tree and collected the lost egg. 'Oh Rabbit, what are we to do now?' asked Mr. Hogg, pushing up his glasses and looking at the egg in his paws.

'If there is thinking that is to be done, then there is only one thing for it.' replied Rabbit.

'What is that?'

'Tea and cake!'

'Oh! Yes, that will help me think.' said Mr. Hogg, who was particularly fond of carrot cake.

'Follow me.' said Rabbit, and, with a tap of his walking stick on the forest floor, headed for the path that led to his burrow beneath the old oak tree.

They walked through the bushes and undergrowth, past the shining snowdrops and patches of bright trumpeting daffodils and clambered down a rocky slope until they reached the path that led back to Rabbit's front door.

There, within his burrow, which was full of books about flowers, plants, herbs and vegetables, they sat beside the fire and drank tea and ate cake, talking and laughing about times gone by, tales of their youth and legends of the forest.

The evening grew darker, and they agreed that a quest could not possibly be completed on an empty stomach, so Rabbit cooked them a most excellent meal, before they settled in their chairs beside the warm fire. Mr. Hogg dozed, drooping, his glasses slipping from his nose. Just before he fell asleep, however, he noticed something odd.

The egg, which had been placed in front of the fire in between their chairs, in one of Rabbit's homemade wicker baskets, twitched . . . and squeaked.

Chapter 2

After a delicious breakfast of poached eggs on buttered toast (don't worry - our egg is safe!) Mr. Hogg and Rabbit left the burrow, heading for the path that led toward the river. They had decided to journey to the riverside, as upon the banks and within the reeds would be ducks and numerous waterfowl. Ducks, they decided, were their next best bet.

Early morning sunshine dappled the path ahead and, despite the cold spring air, the plants and flowers raised their petals in delight. Blackbirds sang and flicked the leaf litter around the forest floor, searching for worms. 'A beautiful morning, my dear Rabbit!' said Mr. Hogg as he strode in front, carrying the egg in his paws.

'A beautiful morning indeed, my dear Mr. Hogg.' replied Rabbit, buttoning his waistcoat and planting each step with his walking stick.

They tracked the path, walking through a forest of curled ferns, climbing over fallen logs covered with green moss. It had been a long time since Mr. Hogg had been this far from home and, despite enjoying the sights and sounds and smells of the spring forest, he was tired and looked forward to going home to his pile of brown leaves. He had much to do to prepare for the coming season. Like Rabbit, Mr. Hogg had his own passions and, when he was not cleaning, eating or strolling, he loved to write novels, especially with quill and ink, usually by candlelight. Short stories were his favourite, although most recently, before hibernation, he had been working on an autobiography: the memoirs of an aging hedgehog, the life and times of the prickly woodland creature.

'Help! Help me!' came a cry from ahead.

Mr. Hogg stopped. 'Did you hear that?' he asked Rabbit.

Rabbit nodded, looking concerned, and they hurried as fast as their paws could carry them.

Climbing around the risen, twisted roots of a very old tree, they found the source of the outcry. A group of crows flapped and jumped around a small lizard, pecking at it, trying to eat it. 'Help!' The lizard cried as the crows cawed.

Mr. Hogg did not delay. Quickly giving the egg to Rabbit to hold, he took off his hat and glasses and popped into a ball! Rolling along, he sped toward the crows and crashed into them one by one. They didn't see him at first, but they certainly felt him.

'Ouch!' yelled the first.

'Ow!' yelled the second.

'Ouuuuch!' yelled the third. 'Let's go!'

With spiky feathers, they took off through the trees, leaving their prey shocked at the change of fate. Mr. Hogg unfurled himself and, with a shake of his spines, he nodded a good riddance to the fleeing crows. He turned to the lizard, 'my dear fellow, are you quite alright? Those crows can be a nasty business.'

'You saved me!' cried the lizard, panting with fright and relief, 'thank you, thank you, a thousand thank you's! Why, if it wasn't for your heroic efforts, I'd have been breakfast for those crows!'

Once Rabbit arrived, Mr. Hogg donned his hat and put on his glasses, seeing

Lizard more clearly. 'Heroic! I say! I thank you for your kind compliment, but I am not a hero; just a small, prickly creature who likes to eat carrot cake.'

'His efforts at tackling carrot cake, too, are also heroic, might I add.' added Rabbit with a smile.

'Allow me to introduce myself – I am Mr. H Hogg, and this is my dear friend, Rabbit.'

Rabbit gave a bow.

Lizard nodded and clasped his paw. 'You are a hero to me, Mr. H Hogg. Thank you. What, might I ask, are you doing out here with a snake's egg?'

'A snake egg?! I say, good heavens!!' exclaimed Mr. Hogg. 'Are you quite sure?'

Lizard nodded. 'I am a reptile, as is the snake, and I can tell you that the egg you're holding is the egg of a reptile.'

'Are you quite sure this is the egg of a snake though? It could be a lizard's egg?' asked Rabbit.

'Hmm.' Lizard crept in for a closer look, then jumped back in fright, 'yes. This is a snake egg!'

Mr. Hogg looked at Rabbit and Rabbit looked at Mr. Hogg. This required some thought. A snake was something different from a bird or a duck; this was a predator. This was dangerous. Although, when he looked down at the egg in his paws, this poor, lost egg without home or parent, he knew he must do something, or at least try. Looking at Rabbit, Mr. Hogg nodded his answer that he was willing to continue. Rabbit replied with a nod in agreement.

It was settled.

'I found this egg when I awoke from hibernation, you see, and we are searching for its home to return it to its parent or guardian. If this egg does indeed belong to a snake, then the snake nest is where we must go. If you do know, would you mind terribly if I asked you for the location of said nest?' asked Mr. Hogg.

Lizard nodded. 'You must cross the stream by the big cedar tree and follow the path down to the darker part of the forest. There you will find rotting logs and slimy rocks. There, beneath one of those logs, you will find the nest of the snake.'

'Very well.' said Mr. Hogg, 'thank you for your help, Lizard. Take care of yourself. Farewell.'

'Goodbye, and good luck, my friend! And thank you once again Mr. H Hogg!' Lizard cried as they turned away, heading for the stream. Lizard then crawled around for a while, searching the ground, 'now, where did my glasses get to?'

As the morning turned into afternoon, Mr. Hogg and Rabbit found the stream by the big cedar tree and clambered over the shallow current by wibbling and wobbling across a small log. Here, upon the bank of the stream, whilst watching the small fish dart beneath and listening to the gentle tinkle of water over rocks, they had their lunch. Neither wanted to think about their destination. Neither liked who they had to meet. The egg had a different feel to it now they knew what lay curled within, yet neither could be swayed to leave it. There is a great honour amongst the creatures of the forest, as I am sure you are aware, and despite knowing that this egg belonged to a predator, they knew they had a duty to keep it safe.

They followed the path through thickets of dried-up ferns and the trunks of tall slim trees, passing a deer that nodded in reply to Mr. Hogg tilting his hat with a 'good afternoon.' The deer hurried along, its stick-legs making light work of the scrub that they struggled through.

Eventually they reached a darker place, a place where the trees were closer together and the air was stuffier and smelled of rot. The ground was covered in old, dead leaves and logs and mushrooms sprouted here, there and everywhere; their little umbrella-like hats bright against the gloom. 'I think we are here, Mr. Hogg.' whispered Rabbit, as if the trees could hear them.

Mr. Hogg nodded but did not reply. He was busy trying to keep his spines from rattling too loudly, which they did when he was either nervous . . . or scared.

They passed a very old tree trunk that was riddled with holes and rips, the bark almost peeling away from the fibrous centre. 'I am not too fond of this place.' admitted Rabbit.

'I suppose our forest will look like this one day, Rabbit. Whilst our forest is young and new and at the start of the circle, this place is at the end. It is just the way things are, my friend. It is only nature.' said Mr. Hogg, trying to help his friend and trying to calm himself too. 'But yes, I am not too fond either.'

After searching for a while, they caught the scent and path of their mission. Their path led them to an old log, rotting, covered in moss and mushrooms. At the bottom, on the ground, was a hole. Small, but big enough for a certain scaly legless reptile.

Building up the courage with a deep breath, Mr. Hogg took a step closer and rapped on the log with a shaking paw. 'Mr. Hogg?' asked Rabbit.

'One moment, Rabbit.' replied Mr. Hogg. There was no answer, so he knocked again.

'Mr. Hogg?' Rabbit tried again, sounding a little more nervous.

After another moment, Mr. Hogg shrugged and guessed that nobody was home. 'Yes?' He turned and saw Rabbit frozen with fear, and a very large, long, stripy snake curled around poor Rabbit's legs. With its smooth head risen from the ground, it looked at Rabbit straight in the eyes and with a long, forked tongue, the snake hissed over Rabbit's face!

'Good grief! Rabbit!!' cried Mr. Hogg. 'Please do not hurt my friend!'

'What's thisss? A rabbit?' said the snake, with eyes that did not blink. 'What isss a rabbit doing ssso far from home?'

Rabbit's ears were folded and low.
'I . . . I . . . H-Hello.' squeaked Rabbit.

Snake hissed a hiss that sounded like
a laugh. It smiled and licked its slimy
lips. 'Hello, little rabbit. It hasss been
a long time sssince I have had visssitors.
How are you?'

Rabbit gulped. 'I . . . I-I have been
better. How are you?'

Snake tilted her head in confusion.
'It hasss been a long time sssince
sssomeone hasss asssked me how I am.
Mossst sssimply run before we can talk.
Even though I am a sssnake, even though
I have a lisssp, I ssstill like to talk. I like
company. To tell you the truth, I get
lonely out here. Nobody likesss to come
to thisss part of the foressst, and nobody
likesss to talk with me.' said Snake.

Strangely, all the fear left Rabbit and
Mr. Hogg, then. Snake was not to be
afraid of. Snake, as Mr. Hogg then

realised, was simply misjudged. He stepped closer and laid a paw upon its scaly back. 'My dear fellow, I apologise for my fear. You frightened us, you see, and I have not come across many friendly snakes. Forgive me for my prejudice. Allow me to introduce myself – I am Mr. H Hogg, at your service.' He took his hat off and gave a bow.

'And I am Rabbit.' said Rabbit and gave a nervous bow.

Snake nodded; her tongue flickered. 'It isss a pleasure to meet you, Mr. H Hogg and Rabbit. What bringsss you to thisss part of the foressst, pray tell?'

Mr. Hogg displayed the egg with outstretched arms. 'We have been on a quest to return this lost egg to its rightful owner, and we have been told that it belongs to you, or your kin, so we have sought you out in order to return what you have been missing.' He placed the egg on the ground and the snake slithered over and smelled the shell with a flicker of her forked tongue.

'I admire your determination, and your honour, Mr. H Hogg. It isss rare for sssomeone to go ssso far out of their way for sssomeone elssse.'

'It is not as rare as you might think. There is kindness everywhere, if only you are open to seeing it.' replied Mr. Hogg.

'Indeed.' said Snake, 'although, I regret to inform you that thisss isss not an egg of mine, nor any of my kin. Thisss isss not a sssnake egg.'

'Oh! Are you sure?' asked Mr. Hogg, confused.

'It is only, we were told that this is most definitely a snake egg.' added Rabbit.

'I am quite sure. By whom where you told?'

'Lizard.'

'Lizard!' hissed the snake, laughing. 'Lizard has famousssly abysssmal eyesssight.'

'Oh!' cried Mr. Hogg. 'Drat! Then our quest is not yet over.'

'I am afraid it isss not. But you cannot continue jussst yet, it isss almost dark! Pleassse, ssstay, dine with me and resume your journey tomorrow.' said Snake.

Mr. Hogg looked to Rabbit, who gulped nervously. 'Just to clarify, when you say "dine", do you mean–?'

Snake laughed and hissed, 'I mean you are not dinner! Come, join me.' She slithered to the hole and disappeared beneath the log. Picking up the still lost egg, Mr. Hogg glanced over it and said, 'don't worry, little egg, we shall get you home.' They followed Snake to the rotten log but before climbing through the hole to the chamber beneath, Rabbit stopped.

'Are you sure about this, Mr. Hogg?' Despite not feeling fearful of Snake, Rabbit could not completely forsake his prejudice of the predator.

Mr. Hogg thought about it for a second, but eventually nodded. 'I think so. She seems friendly enough. But if we do not feel comfortable, we shall excuse ourselves politely and camp elsewhere. Agreed?'

'Agreed.' said Rabbit and thumped the ground in apprehension before following Mr. Hogg down the snake hole. Within, they found a comfortable and roomy underground chamber, and Snake preparing food. There was a table and chair, a bed and a small rug in front of a fire. There was no air of threat, only welcome.

They ate good food and talked about the way of things, about the forest and winter just passed before settling down in front of the fire to sleep. Mr. Hogg stared at the egg as he fell asleep, and the egg stared back at him.

At some point in the night, Mr. Hogg was suddenly awakened by a shaking on the shoulder. 'I am terribly sssorry to wake you, Mr. H Hogg, but there isss sssomething you need to sssee.'

'What is it?' Mr. Hogg asked and sat up, immediately seeing why Snake had woken him. Beside the fireplace, in the glow of the embers, the egg jolted and twitched and rolled upon the floor. Quickly, Mr. Hogg woke Rabbit and they all watched as the egg danced to and fro, kicking from side to side.

Suddenly, with a terrific crack that made them all jump, a foot broke free from the bottom of the egg! Then, after a minute or two, the other foot followed, and the legs wiggled in their newfound freedom. 'Good heavens!' exclaimed Mr. Hogg as the legs found the ground and, with a roll, managed to stand!

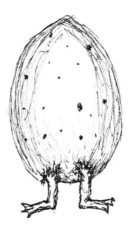

In panic, or perhaps excitement, they were not sure, the egg began to run around them, hopping and jumping, bumping into the table and chair until it lost its footing and fell back on its shell, rolling around on the floor. They laughed and helped to steady it. 'Rabbit, please could you hold the egg whilst I examine the feet. Perhaps they could tell us where we need to visit next.'

Even when Rabbit first held the upper egg, Mr. Hogg could see the main feature of the feet: the three toes were black and were webbed, which told him almost everything he needed to know.

'I do believe, Mr. H Hogg, that your journey liesss toward the river.' hissed Snake.

'I do believe, my dear snake, that you are right.' replied Mr. Hogg.

Chapter 3

The following morning, after a breakfast of nuts and berries (snake's larder was not well suited to Mr. Hogg's and Rabbit's diet – snake did not possess toast or eggs and nowhere was carrot cake to be found, much to Mr. Hogg's dismay) and a hearty farewell from Snake, who seemed much pleased by their compassion and company, they set off from the darker part of the forest, heading toward the river. The difference this morning, however, was that there was no longer a need to carry the egg, for it trotted along beside them with small slapping steps!

Following the path, they found the stream once more but instead of crossing it, they decided to walk along it. Neither had been to the river before, you see, for they had no need to, and both were unsure of how to get there and where to find it. 'Are you quite sure this is the right way?' asked Rabbit.

'I am not sure. I believe it to be.' replied Mr. Hogg, then realised something. If the egg was indeed that of a duck, or goose, or perhaps a swan, then perhaps it knew the way to the river. He turned to find the egg happily trotting along behind them, and he smiled. 'My dear egg, since you seem to belong to that of waterfowl, I don't suppose you would know the way to the river, and whether you could perhaps lead us there? If I may be so bold as to ask.'

The egg stopped walking and stood still. There was no reply. Mr. Hogg stared at the egg, and the egg stared right back.

'Hmm.' said Rabbit, stroking his chin in thought, 'perhaps it does not understand language yet?'

'Indeed. Well, it shouldn't take long, our little egg picked up walking within seconds.'

'Aha! Right you are, Mr. Hogg.'

They continued along the stream, their walking sticks gently prodding the ground with each step and, following closely behind with small slapping steps, was their shelled companion: the egg.

Slowly widening, the stream turned and twisted. Sometimes it became fast flowing rapids over ledges of rock, sometimes it slowed so much so that they could see the underwater world beneath the surface. Branches overhung and intertwined with the branches from the other bank, giving squirrels a perfect route across, and other branches dangled low into the water, providing a perfect nursery for baby fish. As they walked, they pointed out all the beauty they could see, from the underwater grasses swaying in the current, to the kingfisher flitting from branch to stream, then back to the branch with a full beak. They even spotted an otter swimming by. 'Wonderful!' cried Mr. Hogg, 'delightful! I say Rabbit, we shall have to use this walk more often throughout the year, I am sure the scenes here during the hot summers, chilly autumns and cold winters are sublime.'

'Agreed!' agreed Rabbit.

Eventually, the stream became a river, and they passed swathes of tall reeds with bushy heads and marveled at the twisted, old willow tree whose branches were so low that its spindly leaves skimmed the surface of the water. At last, when the sun was beyond noon, they encountered the first nest. It was that of a large grey goose who sat dutifully upon a wide bed of sticks and reeds. 'Hello there. Excuse me, pardon the interruption of your peace, but would you have happened to have lost an egg recently? We have found this poor lost egg and we are searching for its parents. As you can see, it has begun to hatch already.' asked Mr. Hogg from the riverbank. 'My name is Mr. H Hogg, and this is my dear friend, Rabbit.'

Rabbit gave a bow.

The goose unfurled its long neck, looked at the strange trio and smiled. 'I have not lost anything recently, Mr. H Hogg. This egg does not belong to me, although there are more nests along the riverbank that you can try. Perhaps a poor duck or swan has misplaced one.'

Mr. Hogg tipped his hat, 'I thank you for your advice, dear goose, and I wish you all the best for the coming nesting season. Good afternoon.'

Goose nodded, 'And I wish you the best of luck on your mission; it is a truly admirable thing, to go so far for an egg that does not belong to you. Good afternoon.'

For the rest of the afternoon, they marched along the riverbank repeating the same script as the first, questioning whether anyone was the owner of their egg. Unfortunately, no one claimed it; not duck, moorhen or cormorant, and the egg trailed behind them still with its small slapping steps.

They began to lose faith in their expedition to the riverbank. They were confused. The feet were webbed, surely that meant the creature within the shell was a creature bound for the water. As the sun began to lower in the sky and the first hints of evening approached, they encountered a large white swan with patchy feathers around its bald bottom half and tail, sitting upon a floating nest. Its head was tucked under its wing, and they heard it crying.

'Excuse me, my dear swan, are you quite alright?' asked Mr. Hogg.

The swan looked up from its wing and tears rolled down its orange bill. 'I'm sorry you have come across me like this. Usually, I am much stronger and can face things better, but after what has happened, I don't feel I can.'

'There is nothing to apologise for.' said Mr. Hogg, removing his hat, 'when things happen to us that we do not expect, or even like, it is okay to not be strong and it is okay to cry. It shows us that we can mourn for what we have lost, so that we are better able to let things go.'

'What has happened, if you don't mind me asking?' asked Rabbit.

The swan looked down at her bald patches. 'Only yesterday a pike attacked me. I managed to escape but it plucked all the feathers I needed to keep my eggs warm. Oh! How can I care for my young now?' she said, crying.

With a steady hand on the egg so that it did not step too far, they stepped to the edge of the bank. 'How awful that such a thing has happened!' cried Rabbit, 'we are here for you, and we will do all we can to help.'

Swan smiled, 'thank you, my friends. There is nothing that can be done. I am a fine knitter, you see, I could knit a blanket to keep myself and my eggs warm, but I do not have any needles. I suppose I shall have to wait and try again next spring.'

Just then, Mr. Hogg had a brilliant idea. Reaching behind, he picked two of his longest, strongest spines and snapped them free. 'Here, take these. Use them and knit a blanket for yourself and your young.' He reached out and Swan, shocked and touched, took them with her bright orange bill.

'I am overcome with happiness! Oh, thank you, Mr. H Hogg! Thank you! Now I can make a blanket and give my babies the best start in life.' Honked Swan.

'Speaking of your young,' said Rabbit, 'have you, by any chance, misplaced one? We are searching the riverbank for this fellow's home, and, as you can see, it has already begun to hatch! We have checked with every other nest nearby and none have lost anything.'

Swan shook her head, 'I am terribly sorry, but this is not my egg, either. I only lost my feathers, not any of my eggs. Are you sure this is the egg of a waterbird?'

'Its feet are webbed; we assumed that it must be so.' replied Rabbit.

'How curious!' honked Swan, looking at the egg with its two legs poking out. 'Perhaps it is not a bird.'

'Then what could it be?'

Swan thought for a moment, then replied: 'I'm not sure, but I know of someone who might be able to help. I shall call my partner and he will be able to take you.' She then called over to her partner who swam to the nest and, after telling him what had happened, he agreed to take them.

Carefully, Mr. Hogg, Rabbit and the egg climbed upon the swan's back, and, with powerful strokes, it took off from the bank and into the current of the river. 'Thank you ever so much!' called Mr. Hogg to the nesting swan as they drifted away.

'Of course! And thank you, Mr. H Hogg!' called Swan.

With its feet giving powerful strokes and its wings fluffed up, the ride was comfortable, and they moved quickly. They passed thick reeds with chattering warblers and tiny voles swimming back to their riverbank holes. The sun began to set by the time the swan drifted over to the opposite riverbank where a path cut through the reeds. 'This is as close as I can get you. If you follow this path, it will lead you past a very old oak tree and when you get there, call for Old Owl. He will be able to help you.'

They disembarked onto the path, 'Thank you so much, my good swan!' said Mr. Hogg.

He bowed his head. 'This is the least I could do for you helping my wife and children. The honour is all mine, Mr. H Hogg.' Then he turned and swam upstream back to his family, perched upon their pontoon.

They followed the path as it took them away from the river and through a grassy clearing, gently prodding the way with their walking sticks. Pheasants called loudly to each other as they roosted, and flocks of starlings swirled and twisted into the evening sky. 'I am so excited!' said Rabbit, 'I have only heard of the wisdom of Old Owl, but now I get to meet him!'

'Yes, it will be good to meet him. I hope he has some answers for us.' Despite the adventure, the truth of it was that Mr. Hogg missed home. He was tired. He wished to settle down in front of a fire with a blanket on his lap and a cup of tea within reach, (with, perhaps, some biscuits of course) reading an excellent book. But he knew he would not be able to rest until the egg had been returned home. Whenever he looked upon it now, waddling behind them, he smiled.

'I have thought of a name for our dear fellow companion,' said Rabbit, 'Mr. E – E for egg, and because Mr. E sounds exactly like mystery! Which is exactly what it is!' Rabbit laughed.

Mr. Hogg laughed too, 'Oh how excellent! Very clever, I like it.'

As the shadows grew longer and night began, they encountered a very large, old oak tree. Its trunk was huge and gnarled, its branches low and widespread. 'I think we have found it.' said Rabbit with a grin, showing his large front teeth. 'I wonder if Owl is at home.' Rabbit called out, called up, and waited.

Eventually, a head popped out of a hole in the trunk. 'Who? Who?' (It has been said amongst the creatures of the forest that Owl is the oldest of owls and their trademark hoot originated from this particular owl who, with his age, had become increasingly hard of hearing.) 'Who goes there?'

'We are terribly sorry to interrupt your evening, kind sir. My name is Rabbit, and this is my dear friend Mr. H Hogg. We have something here we need your help with; something that might interest you.'

'Oh! Is that so? I do like things that interest me, and I do hope that this lives up to expectation! Please, come on up.' hooted Old Owl.

Rabbit looked up and down the trunk, confused. 'Erm . . . how do we do that?'

'By the stairs of course!' laughed Owl. And when they checked around the back of the trunk (if there is such a thing), they found a small door and upon opening it, found a spiraling staircase that led all the way up the tree! They climbed it, helping the egg with the steps until they came upon Owl's home. It was small and cosy, with a table and chairs beside the window and a perch above the rounded, stacked bookcase that lined the inner trunk. Books were everywhere, about everything and everyone. If there was a place to get answers; this was it.

'Mr. Rabbit, Mr. H Hogg – a pleasure. My name is Owl. Some have also referred to me as Old Owl or Old Tawny,

but you can call me Owl.' He shook
their paws with a wing. 'And what do
we have here? An egg in the process
of hatching, with the feet of a duck – I
am not sure you needed my help in
finding who this egg belongs tooo-tooo.'
Owl hooted.

'Indeed, we thought so too. Until
today. We checked along the riverbank,
and none claimed it. All confirmed that
this is not a duck, goose or swan egg.
We even checked with the moorhens
and cormorants.' explained Mr. Hogg,
taking off his hat. He then told Owl
of their journey, who they had come
across, who they had asked.

'I see! Quite the journey for two
mammals who have no relation nor
connection to eggs. But a wonderous
journey indeed!' Owl stooped for a
closer look, the egg reflecting in his
big, bright eyes. 'How interesting . . .

An egg that does not appear to belong to any species that lays eggs. And for the sake of elimination; this is not an owl egg either.'

'Do you know what this egg is? Where it belongs or who it belongs to?' asked Rabbit.

Owl stood and stroked his beak in thought. 'I have heard tales of a mysterious creature roaming the forest, an ancient creature that does not seem to fit into any species. A missing link, if you will. Then again, I am an academic. I thought it to be nothing more than foolishness, poppycock – gobbledygook. And yet here we are, with an egg with the feet of a duck that is not a duck and a stack of unanswered questions: oh, how a mystery does wet the tongue for a delicious bite of knowledge!' Owl turned and began to search the bookcases with interest, skimming the spines with long grey feathers. 'I believe I may have something here, it will take some time, but rest assured we shall find the owner, whooo-whoooever it is. Please, rest, while I find what I need. There is some tea in the teapot, freshly brewed and freshly baked scones, if you so wish.'

'Oh excellent!' cried Mr. Hogg and they sat themselves at the table, sorting the crockery, preparing the tea and scones. They were famished! The egg, unsure of what to do, plopped itself down on the floor, its legs spread and toes playfully kicking.

There was silence in the trunk for a time whilst Owl sifted through his enormous collection of books, and Mr. Hogg and Rabbit ate and drank their fill. At length, Rabbit said, 'I say, Mr. Owl, it is wonderful to meet you. I have only heard tales of your wisdom and knowledge.'

Owl smiled, 'too many seem to confuse the two, I'm afraid, and prioritise one above the other. Knowledge is only a part of it, but in my many years I have learned that there are, in fact, four main pillars of wisdom: knowledge, patience, kindness and love. Each are equal to each other in this worthy pursuit. But I will say this unto you, Mr. Rabbit, the pursuit of wisdom often does not lead to it. It must grow naturally, as this oak tree did. Day by day, year by year, century by century; a nurturing enterprise that led it to touch the sky, as you will too.' Owl nodded, 'and, might I add, it is wonderful to meet you tooo-tooo.'

'The feeling is mutual, Mr. Owl, and I thank you for the inspiring advice, and delicious scones.' said Mr. Hogg.

After a time and after much scouring, Owl decided he did not have the book he needed in his collection and had to visit another of his tree-trunk homes to check the bookcases there. He would not be long, he assured them. Away Owl flapped into the night, leaving Mr. Hogg, Rabbit and the egg alone.

'I wish I could be as wise as Mr. Owl one day.' Rabbit said as they sat talking by candlelight.

'Well, Rabbit, you have knowledge, you are patient, you are kind, and you are loved; I would say you're already wise, my good friend. You don't need to change anything. You are enough.' replied Mr. Hogg with a smile.

'Mr. Hogg! You are too kind, let's be wise together.'

'I do believe that is the best kind of wisdom.'

Just then there was a loud squeak and a crackle that made them both startle. Such strange noises, and they came from the egg! It jolted and twisted just as it did before, and the little legs kicked as if it were trying to push away or push out. 'Good heavens! Rabbit, look!'

Suddenly there was a loud crack and an arm popped free, followed by the other only a moment later. The egg pushed itself up and looked around as if it could see, giving an expression of bewilderment if it had a face to do so – it was a look that said, "what on earth happened there?"

Mr. Hogg was overjoyed and immediately reached out and shook the free hand. It was still damp and sticky, with short brown fur and black webbed paws. 'Well done, dear egg! Well done! A marvelous job indeed!'

'You're so close! I think one more push ought to do it,' cried Rabbit, shaking the other hand.

'Why, what have we here?' said Owl as he flew in through the window, clutching a very old book in his claws. 'Some new limbs have broken free! Oh, bravo, little egg! It certainly is a mission escaping from the fortress that is the eggshell, I remember it well, even though it was . . . Well, it was many years ago now.' hooted Owl and leaned in closer, 'I say, little egg, we are having some trouble identifying you. Without further dallying, allow me to ask, do you happen to know what you are? Who – who you are?'

All eyes focused on the egg with its four odd limbs and they held their breaths, as in a grand motion, the egg's arms lifted . . . and shrugged.

'I see. Well, perhaps we can gather some more information from my book.' Owl then opened the covers and leafed through the pages. 'Oh, drat these old eyes, they are not what they were.' He blinked uncomfortably.

Mr. Hogg removed his glasses and passed them to Owl. 'Try these on, Mr. Owl.'

Owl slipped on the glasses and suddenly marveled at the world around him, his eyes wide and bright, seeing things for the first time. 'Mr. H Hogg, this is stupendous! Fantastical! Oh, how wonderful a sense sight is! Thank you, my friend!' He took Mr. Hogg's paw and shook it enthusiastically. Then, leaning back over his book, with an aha! immediately found what he had been looking for. 'This entry states that this mysterious creature has only been sighted briefly, so briefly that it has been mistaken as false and regarded as a myth. Those that have seen it say it has the paws of an otter, the tail of a beaver and the beak of a duck – a missing link between species, how interesting! I wonder if this egg belongs to this strange species.'

'Indeed! I don't think I have ever seen such an animal before. Does your book happen to say where these sightings were?' asked Mr. Hogg, squinting.

'Hmm. It says these sightings were many years ago, around a hidden pond, deep in the woods . . . oh I think I know this area!' Owl then proceeded to tell them how to get there and they agreed to set off on the two day walk at daybreak.

They stayed in Owl's tree trunk for the night, sleeping restlessly; they could barely contain their excitement that they were going to get this poor egg home. In the morning, Owl saw them off from the base of the spiraling staircase at the bottom of the tree. 'All the best for your journey ahead, my good friends, may you have fine weather and good fortune. Oh, and Mr. H Hogg, here are your glasses.' Owl took them off.

Mr. Hogg smiled and held up a paw, 'keep them, my good Owl. I have a spare pair at home.'

'My dear Mr. H Hogg! I am forever grateful, thank you!'

'Farewell, Owl, may we meet again.' Mr. Hogg then shook a wing and they set off, following a small path that was to hopefully take them to the hidden pond and their journey's end.

Chapter 4

To aid in their quest, Owl had
drawn a map for them with distinct
landmarks to follow and at noon, they
stopped for lunch at the first. It was a
large round boulder resting at the base
of a large tree and upon its crest was
a carpet of moss that small flowers
and plants grew from, like a tiny
ecosystem.

'You know, Rabbit, despite having
lived in the same forest all my life, I
continue to be dazzled and impressed
by new and beautiful things that I have
never seen before.' said Mr. Hogg. 'Life
is full of wonderful things.'

Rabbit smiled and raised the cup from
his flask of tea. 'Indeed, it is, Mr. Hogg.'
And they drank.

The map followed the path well and they did not lose their way at all. They passed through fern thickets and climbed over fallen logs, zig-zagged their way down leaf-strewn slopes and waded through shallow streams. The egg marched beside them, gently prodding the ground with its own walking stick now and even though it did not yet have a mouth to participate in discussions, or eyes to wonder at the world, they were glad to have it beside them. To them, it did not need these things to feel like a companion.

At the end of the first day, they made camp in the hollow of a long dead tree. They cooked a wonderful vegetable stew and ate it by the fire, listening to the birds roosting in the branches above and, from somewhere nearby, a tawny owl twitted and twooed. As they watched the embers float from the flames like fireflies, Rabbit produced a flute from his travelling bag and played a tune everyone in the forest knew well. It was a tune that changed like the seasons; a tune that was slow to start, building tempo, until a joyous and catchy crescendo, before slowing and stopping with the same notes – it sang of the growth and decay of the forest, of the great circle of life that all played a part of; from trees to plants, hedgehogs and rabbits. Afterwards, they tucked the egg under a blanket, before sliding under their own blankets and wishing each other a goodnight.

The second day's walk was harder than the first; the landscape changed, and the trees thickened, the slopes were steeper and the streams deeper. Clouds passed over and rain fell, making the path slippery. They pushed on though, glad for their walking sticks and the map that guided them. The landmarks Owl had drawn were peculiar, yet they were accurate when they approached. There was a tree stump that had a sapling growing from it, there was a rock in the shape of a fox and a small waterfall that fell into a pool filled with water lilies. Noon came and went, and their map spoke of two more landmarks before the hidden pool. A huge redwood with roots like buttresses and a small stone circle, so old that even the ancient creatures cannot remember when it came to be.

With aching legs, they came upon the huge redwood roots in the late afternoon and decided to camp within the nook of one of the roots. They cooked a hearty meal before turning in for the night; tomorrow was the big day.

At the first glimmer of dawn, they packed their things and set off with a determined stride. Thankfully the path was visible as it began to wind around trees, switching back to avoid a rocky drop, and disappear and reappear again a little way ahead. They did not talk much, as each was trying to focus on the path, and focus on not crying at their parting with the egg. They had grown to love it and it saddened them that they were not going to see its bobbing shell anymore.

At last, they passed the stone circle, standing in a small clearing atop a hillock. A bizarre thing, so old and mysterious, but they did not dither and continued until they came upon a slope where they gradually clambered down to the bottom. Birds sang loudly and deer raised their heads from the undergrowth, and there was a plop and a croak as a frog jumped into water somewhere nearby.

They pushed through a curtain of vines and saw a large pool bathed in sunlight. Thick reeds bearded the banks and herons stalked the shallows for fish. Ducks bobbed upon the surface and deer drank peacefully. The surrounding trees were old, touched by nothing but time; nature had claimed the forest for its own. They were amazed, this looked like paradise. 'I think we have found our hidden pool.' said Mr. Hogg.

They decided to walk its perimeter, questioning the local wildlife if any had seen any peculiar creatures nearby. All answered with a no, until one answered with a yes. It was a frog, sitting upon a log that nodded, 'I have seen strange creatures here before.' It croaked, 'I was swimming at the time. I swim a lot, you see, I try to swim five laps of the pond a day as part of my training,' (frog was in fact keeping in shape for any passing princesses that might take a shine to its muscles and want a kiss. Anyway, pardon my interruption – let's hear what the frog saw,) 'and it was only the other day when I saw a strange creature in pursuit. It had the bill of a duck, but it was below the surface; it had fur, not feathers and an odd tail, like a beaver. Now, there aren't any beavers here to my knowledge, no otters either, so I leapt from the water, terrified! Us frogs are always on the menu.'

'My, my, that does sound frightening! Where did this occur?' asked Rabbit.

'Over there,' pointed frog with a slimy finger, 'be careful!'

'We shall, thank you.' said Mr. Hogg and they walked a little further . . . and saw them. Swimming and playing in the water, at the deeper end of the pool, were flashes of these fabled creatures. They splashed with their beaver-like tails, shot through the water with incredible speed and pulled up waterweeds with their ducklike bills. 'I believe we are here.' Then, in a flash, they all disappeared.

Just then, they heard crying nearby and upon inspection, they discovered a larger version, sitting on the bank, watching the young frolic in the water, and Mr. Hogg carefully approached. 'Excuse me.' The creature turned to look at him with tears rolling from its black eyes. 'My name is Mr. H Hogg, and this is my good friend Rabbit,'

Rabbit gave a bow and Mr. Hogg recounted their tale from the beginning, and, at the end, he held the egg's paw and led it to the crying animal who leapt up and then took a tentative step forward, as if scared to hope.

'I lost my egg.' It said, 'I thought it had been . . . well, I assumed the worst, for a long time.'

'Is this your egg?' asked Mr. Hogg.

The creature nodded and smiled as another tear rolled down its bill. 'I could recognise the pattern anywhere. Thank you, oh thank you both for all you have done to return my precious egg.'

Mr. Hogg smiled a happy but sad smile and nodded, satisfied. His quest, his adventure, had reached its end. He faced the egg and, with a tear rolling down his cheek, he hugged its shell. 'Goodbye, little egg. Thank you for a wonderful adventure. It has been a pleasure to get to know you over these past few days. You are home.' He took off his hat and placed it atop the egg's peak.

The egg reached up, took it, and held the hat to its centre where its chest was within.

Rabbit then hugged the egg and said farewell, wiping away his own tears.

'With your permission, I would like to visit from time to time, if that would be acceptable?' asked Mr. Hogg.

'Of course! Of course, you would be more than welcome to.' replied the creature.

'Very well then.' He gave a bow, 'then I say unto you, farewell.'

'Goodbye, Mr. H Hogg, and goodbye Rabbit. Thank you once more.' said the creature, holding onto the egg's little paw.

They turned and began the long journey home, but then Mr. Hogg stopped and turned back urgently. 'I almost forgot to ask, if I may be so bold, what creature are you? I have a dear friend who would greatly like to know, as well as myself.'

The creature nodded. 'I am a platypus.'

Mr. Hogg bowed once more, 'it is a pleasure to make your acquaintance, Platypus.' They turned and headed back to the path and, after one last wave, disappeared back through the curtain of vines.

The journey home did not take as long as the outgoing quest, but it felt lonelier, as if they had lost something, and much quieter, even though the egg did not utter a word. After a few days of walking, they stopped by Owl's home on the way and informed him of the egg's safe return and of its species, of which he was overjoyed on both accounts. There, they enjoyed a rest with plentiful chat, tea and scones. Owl told them how much reading he had now been able to do since his restoration of sight and couldn't thank Mr. Hogg enough.

They set off once again, heading for home. The sky was cloudy, and the air had a chill to it; a stiff breeze rattled the reeds as they reached the river and walked along it. Passing the many nests along the riverbank, they felt a mixture of emotion; joy at the completion of their quest but sad that it had led to their dear friend's return home. Of course, they were happy for the little egg, and this happiness helped to ease the pain of its absence. There were no more little slapping steps behind them now, and the world felt that little more overcast.

Reaching the log that served as a bridge, they crossed it, remembering their meeting with the snake, before passing the point at which they had rescued the lizard. They camped under a great leaning rock that night and, in the morning, headed for Rabbit's burrow.

All was as they had left it, yet so much felt different. Nonetheless, it was a joy to see a familiar sight at last. 'Well, this is me.' said Rabbit, opening the front door, 'would you care for a cup of tea before you head home?'

'That sounds perfect.' replied Mr. Hogg and they enjoyed a rest beside the fire with some lunch. After a time, Mr. Hogg decided it was time for him to return home too and they embraced. 'I shall see you soon, my dear friend. Thank you for accompanying me all the way and back again.'

'Of course, Mr. Hogg. The pleasure is mine; it has been a wonderful adventure. Please, drop by anytime for tea and cake.'

'It would be rude to refuse such a delicious offer.' replied Mr. Hogg with a smile, and with a wave, he followed the path that led to his pile of leaves. He had missed it terribly and was now excited to return, to begin his spring cleaning and continue with his memoir.

Rounding the last bend, smelling all the familiar scents that welcomed him home, Mr. Hogg walked with a spring in his step, looking forward to the coming season, to the year ahead. This summer was to be a good one; he had a feeling about it.

Then he stopped in his tracks. And fell to his knees. The sight before him took his breath away.

Sometime before, within the past few days, a large branch had broken from the tree above and had landed on his leaf-litter home. Leaves were scattered everywhere, as was his furniture and the pages of his book, blowing freely in the breeze. 'My home.' uttered Mr. Hogg as he stepped to what had been his front door. He picked up the leaves and let the wind take them from his paws. He picked up the painting of his dear parents – what was left of it. He picked up his quill and a page of his book, crumpled and smudged. It was all gone. Mr. Hogg fell to his knees and rested a paw on the branch that had destroyed his home, and wept.

There was nothing that could be done, except start again. But not yet, his loss was too fresh. After a while, sifting through the pieces, he got to his feet and walked. And walked. And walked.

Mr. Hogg walked back to the stream and sat on the bank, listening to the trickle of water. The sun broke through the clouds and made the surface sparkle. A tear dropped from his little black nose and plopped into the water, where a fish then rose, swimming against the current, looking at him with its glassy eyes. 'Excuse me, are you quite alright?' asked the fish.

'I'll be alright,' said Mr. Hogg, 'I have just learned that my home has been destroyed. I am taking a moment to myself to mourn my loss-'

'So that you can start again?'

'Precisely.'

'Of all the healers, time is the greatest.' said the fish, 'and, like this stream, we don't know what is coming around the bend. All we can do is swim the bend as best as we can. I am glad to be here with you, to share in your moment of loss. Is there anything I can do to help you?'

'Thank you. You are a very kind fish, but no.'

'Always remember, you are never alone.' said the fish and before he could reply, the fish swam away downstream.

Mr. Hogg took a moment before getting to his feet and making his way to Rabbit's burrow where Rabbit welcomed him, consoled him and joined in his sorrow. 'Stay, Mr. Hogg. Stay as long as you need.'

And Mr. Hogg stayed as long as he felt he needed to, grateful for the shelter and friendship, and after four days had passed, four wholesome days full of good food, good company and good gardening with Rabbit, he felt he had healed enough to move on. It was time to start building his new home. It was time to start again.

Chapter 5

'Allow me to help you rebuild.' offered Rabbit and Mr. Hogg accepted. They walked back toward the scene of the destruction, arm in arm, taking slow and steady steps. Mr. Hogg almost couldn't look up to the scene again, he kept his eyes down for as long as possible, until Rabbit said, 'it's time, Mr. Hogg.'

Mr. Hogg looked up and gasped, falling to his knees. 'Why, Rabbit, look!' There, where the branch had fallen, was a brand-new thatch-roofed cottage, complete with a chimney, a garden and a front porch. Smoke rose from the chimney and the windows were alight with a homely glow.

'Everyone. It's time.' Rabbit called, and one by one, all the creatures of the forest they had encountered, all the animals they had helped, stepped out in front of the cottage. Robin flittered down from a branch, Lizard scurried, followed by Snake, Swan and Owl. All smiled and bowed. 'We were terribly sorry to hear what had happened to your home, Mr. H Hogg.' said Owl, 'so we all chipped in and built you a new one, as a way of saying thank you for all you did to help us.'

'You gave us all you had,' said Swan, 'even the spines off your back.' She smiled, showing off a freshly knitted blanket that was knotted around her neck and covered her patchy plumage.

'You gave us friendship.' said Snake.

'You gave us a chance.' said Robin.

'You saved us.' said Lizard.

Mr. Hogg welled up with tears, 'my friends, I did all these things without any expectation of repayment. I helped you because you needed help.'

'And we have helped you because you needed our help.' They said.

'Although, we couldn't have done it without a certain someone who brought us all together as soon as he heard what had happened.' said Rabbit.

'Who is that?' asked Mr. Hogg.

They all smiled and parted to show the cottage. The front door opened and out walked a small platypus, duck-billed, otter-pawed and beaver-tailed. The egg had hatched. Within each of his paws was an item of great importance. A pair of large, round glasses and a hat. 'Me. I came as soon as the fish told me what had happened.' said Platypus. 'It is wonderful to meet you, at last, Mr. Hogg.'

Shocked, Mr. Hogg slipped on his glasses, reached out and embraced Platypus and Platypus embraced him back. 'My dear Platypus! It is excellent to see you and wonderful to meet you at last! What about your mother?' Mr. Hogg cried.

'She understood everything, she said I needed to find my destiny, and being your friend is a part of that journey.' replied Platypus.

'But we took you home!' Mr. H Hogg cried, with tears streaming down his face.

Platypus smiled, wiping away his own tears. 'I am home.'

That night, they all celebrated with a grand feast within the cottage, each sharing tales of their lives and of the forest. They laughed, they ate, they danced to Rabbit's flute and in the morning, each friend bade a fond farewell, inviting Mr. Hogg, Rabbit and Platypus to visit their homes anytime.

The first morning of many inside his new thatch-roofed cottage was spent in a way that Mr. Hogg loved, in fact, he could not think of any better. He sat with Rabbit and Platypus in the spring sunshine upon the front porch, drinking a fine cup of tea and eating a slice of homemade carrot cake, which, as it turns out, Platypus also loved. 'Mmm! This is delicious!' cried Platypus, 'it was most frustrating to hear you both eating delicious food when my mouth had not yet hatched.'

Mr. Hogg laughed, 'you poor thing! I believe I would struggle too if everyone else was eating carrot cake and I could not.'

'You know, Mr. Hogg, I have known you for many years and I have regrettably only now thought to inquire; what does the H stand for? What, indeed, is your first name?' asked Rabbit.

'What do you think it means?' laughed Mr. Hogg.

'Hedge?'

'A fine guess, but no. My name is Horatio, after my grandfather whose spines were so long, it has been said, that he could have passed as a porcupine!'

'Whatever is a porcupine?' laughed Rabbit.

'I have no idea! I suppose we shall have to have another adventure to find out.' laughed Mr. Hogg.

'And next time, hopefully I can be a bit more helpful!' laughed Platypus.

They laughed, and ate their cake and drank their tea, as the birds sang their sweet songs and the sun warmed new flowers into bloom. He smiled at Platypus, and Platypus smiled back. It was going to be a good year, thought Mr. Hogg; he had a feeling about it.

About the Author

I live in Cambridgeshire, and I work as a full-time bricklayer. When I am not building, I am writing books, but this is not my only passion. I also enjoy daily yoga and to paint when I can, and to go for walks in the countryside. I also volunteer at a hedgehog hospital, caring for sick and injured hedgehogs. I love nature and I believe it should be cared for, enjoyed, admired and helped when it needs help.

Ingram Content Group UK Ltd.
Milton Keynes UK
UKHW011136270623
424104UK00001B/22